D0281004

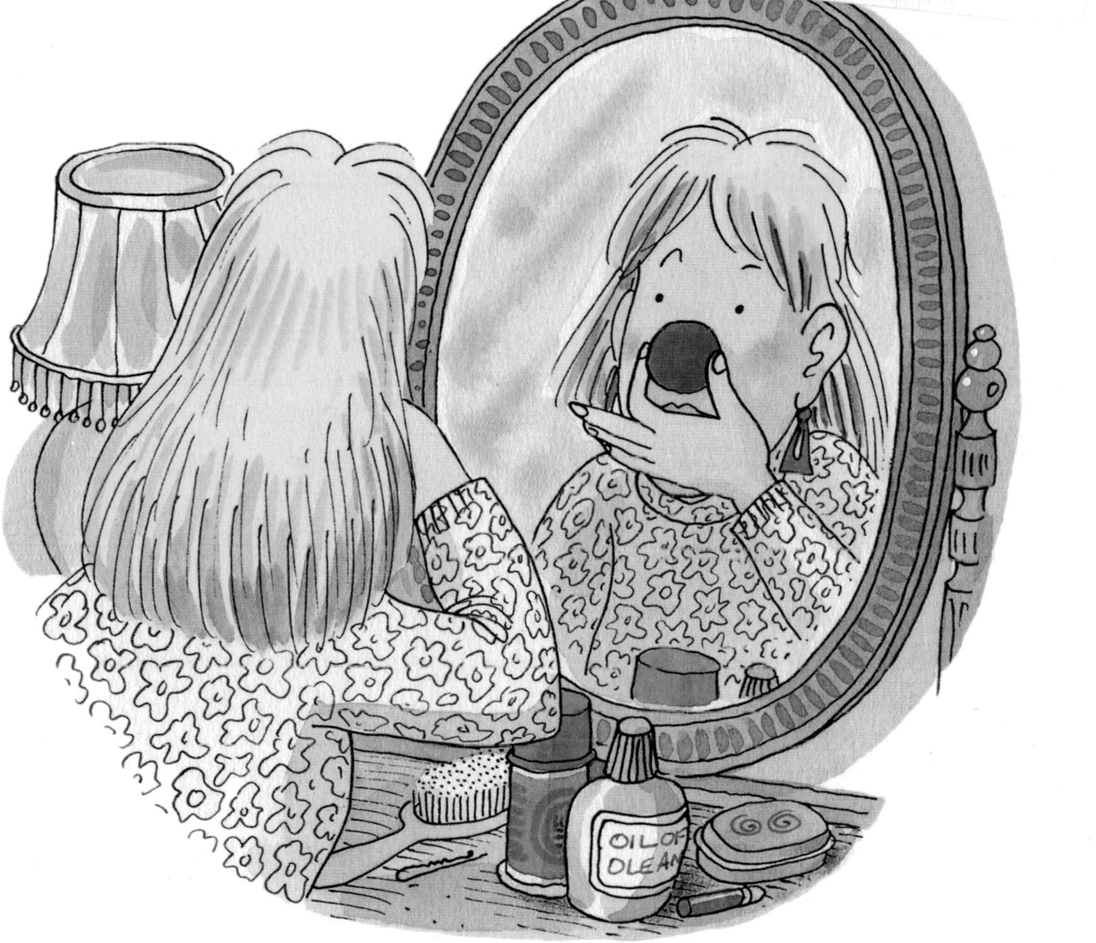

Mum put on a big red nose.

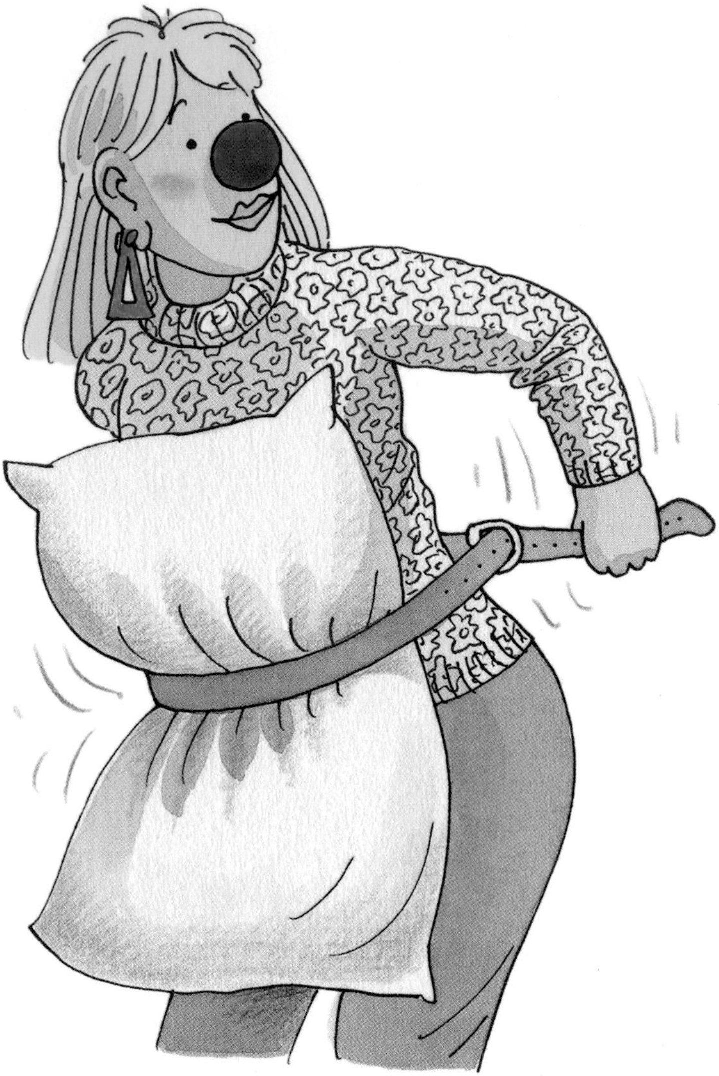

Mum put on a big pillow.

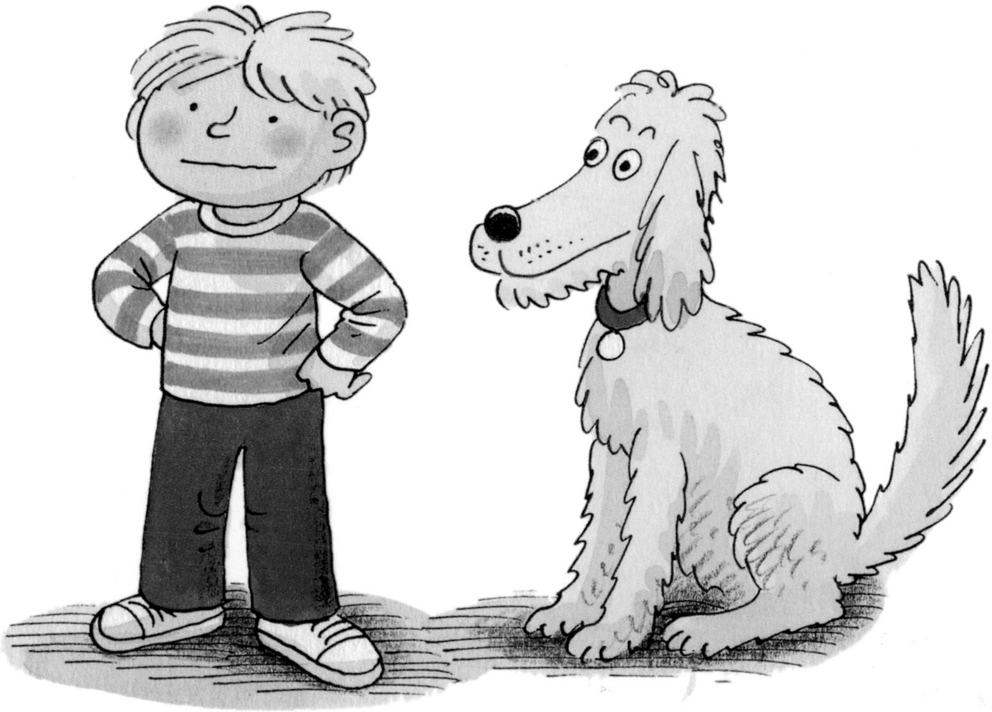

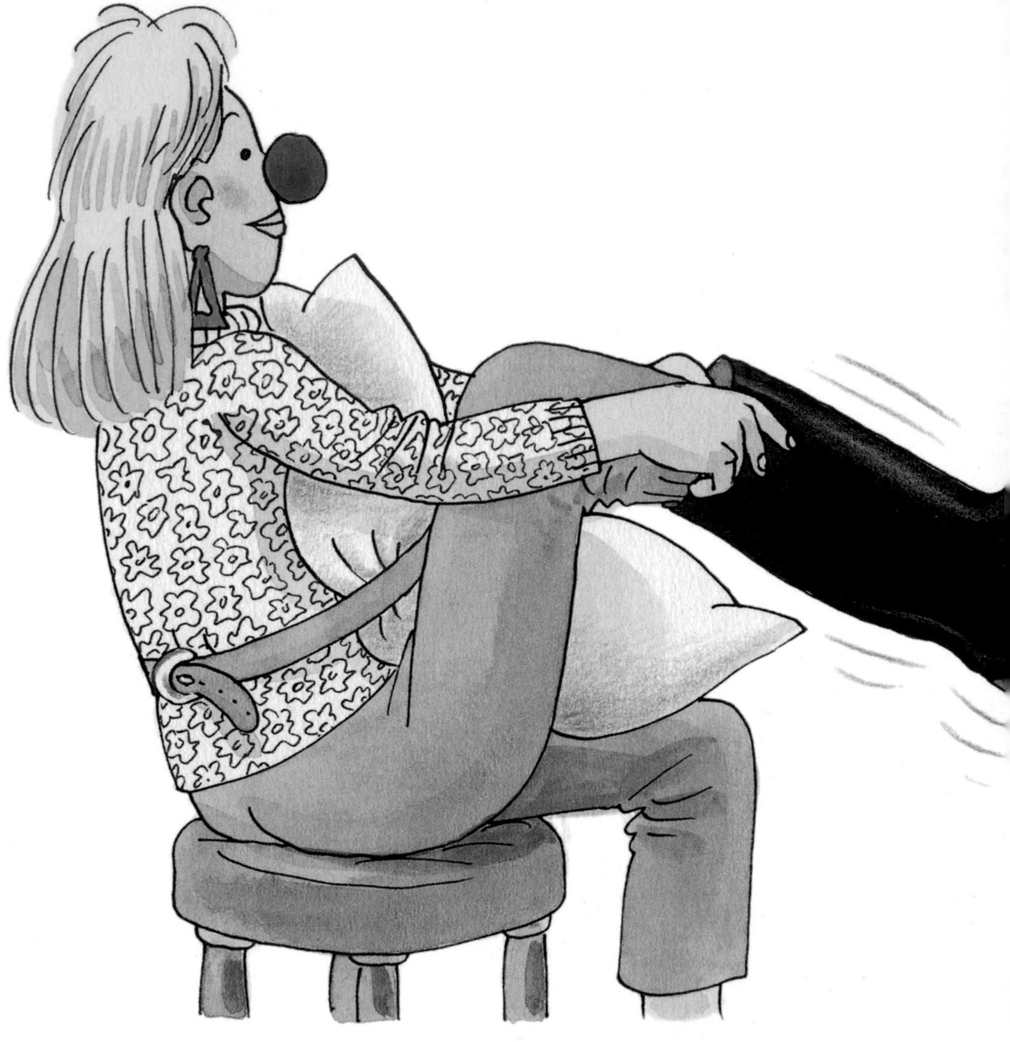

Mum put on big boots.

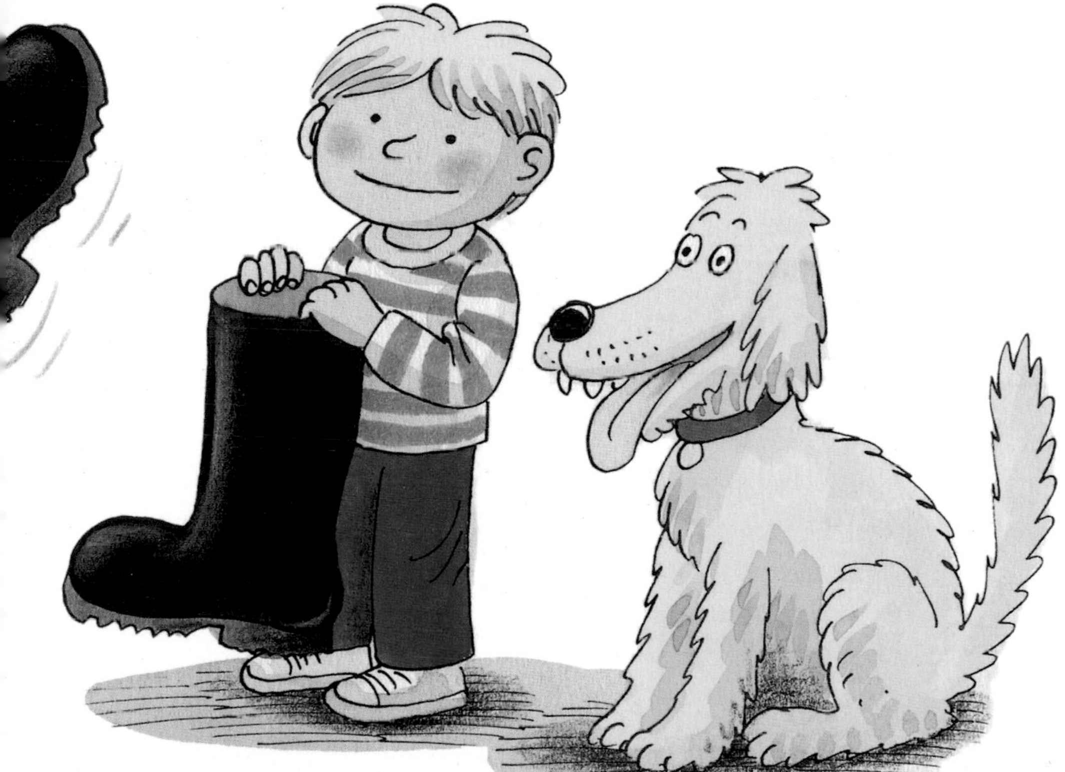

Mum put on big eyebrows.

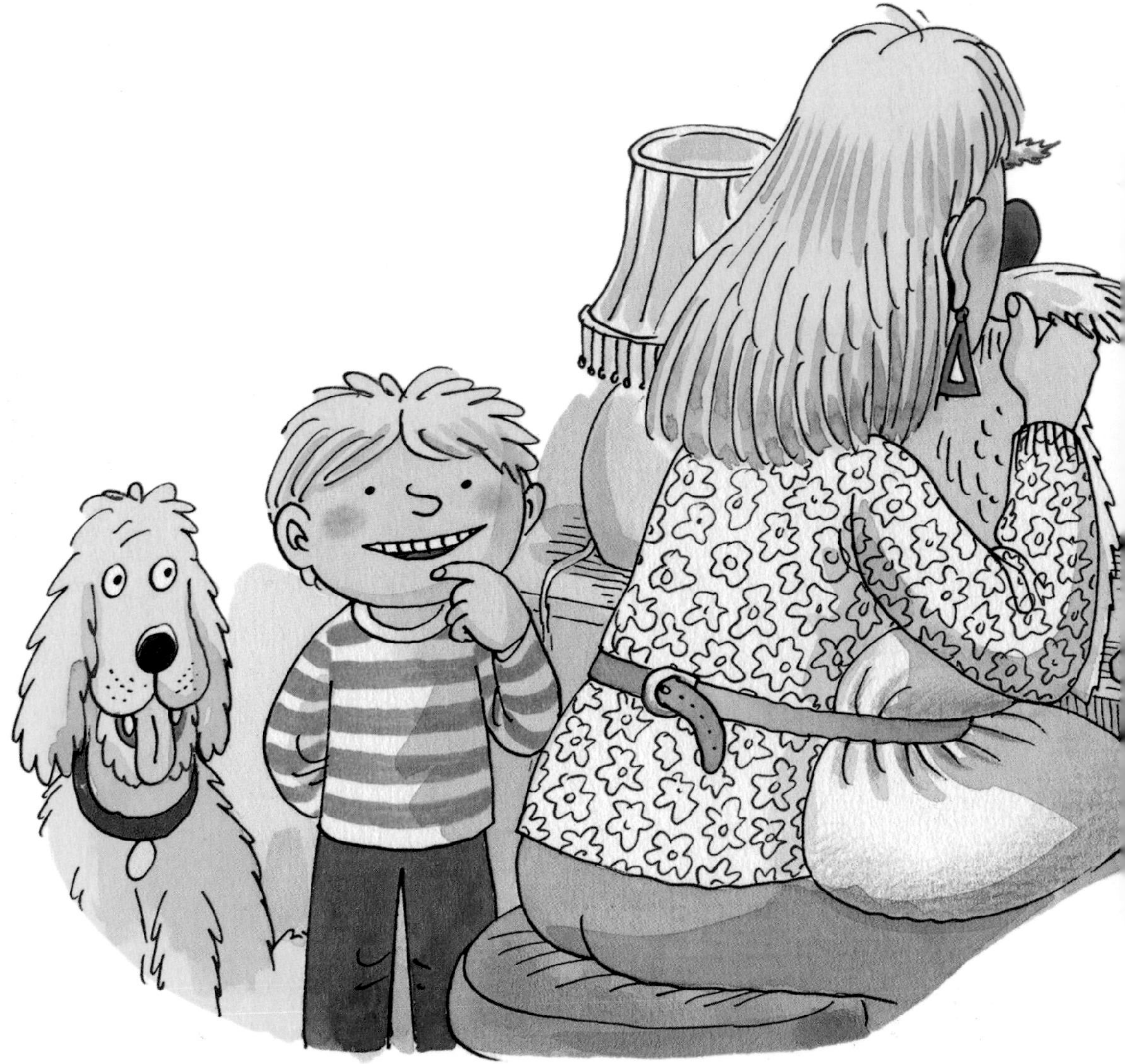

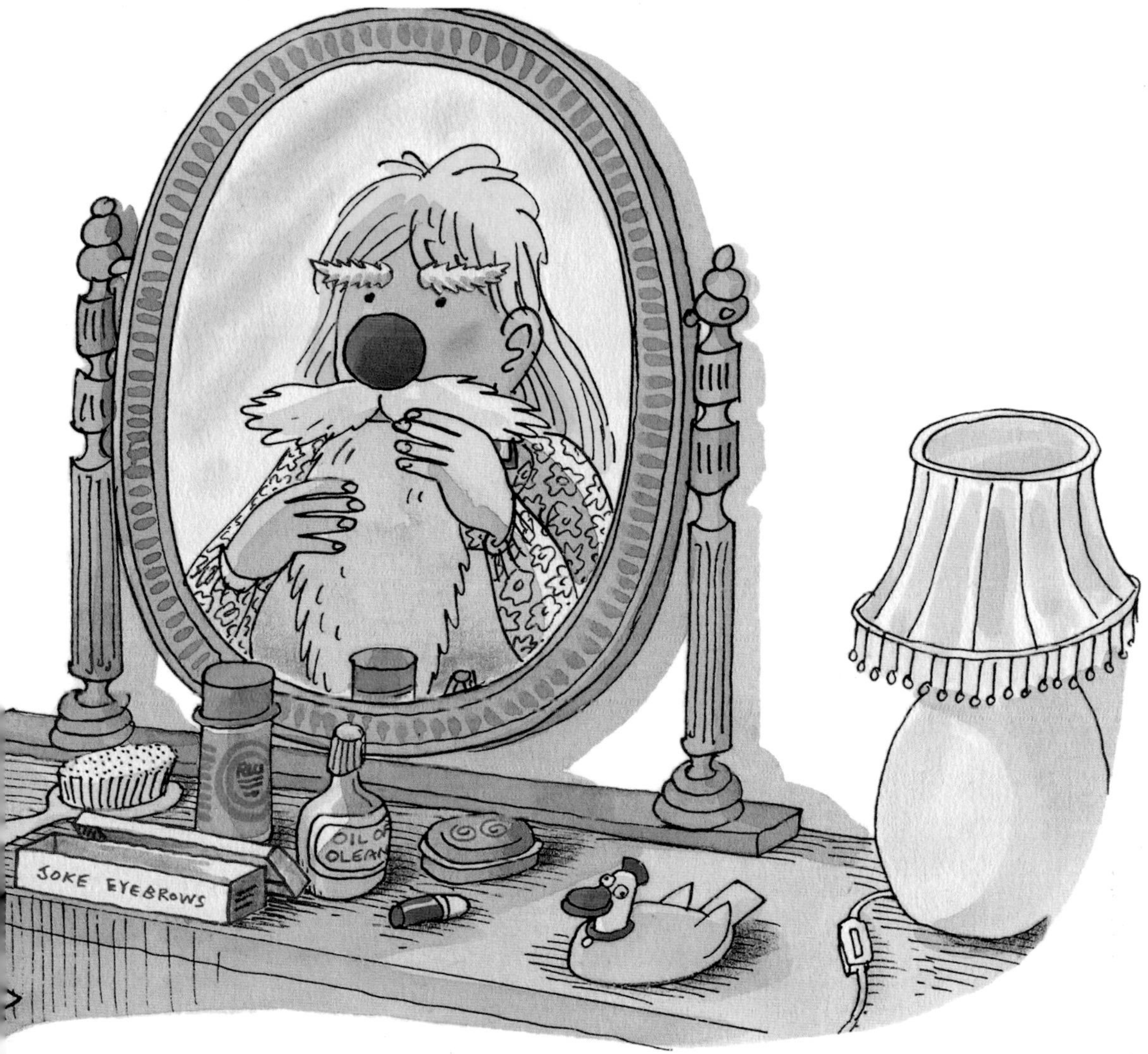

She put on a big beard.

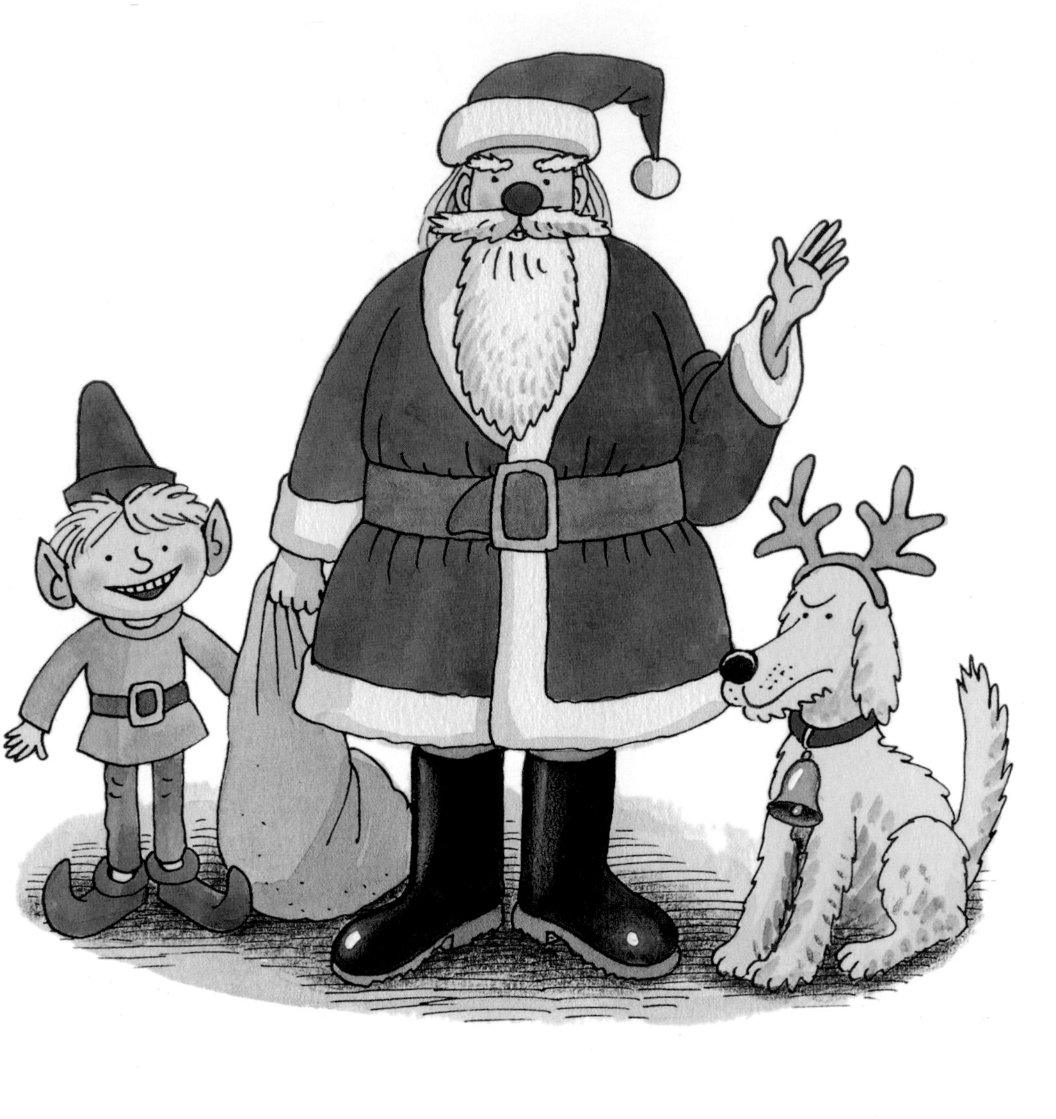

"Ho! Ho! Ho!" said Mum.